DISCARD

The Earth Gnome

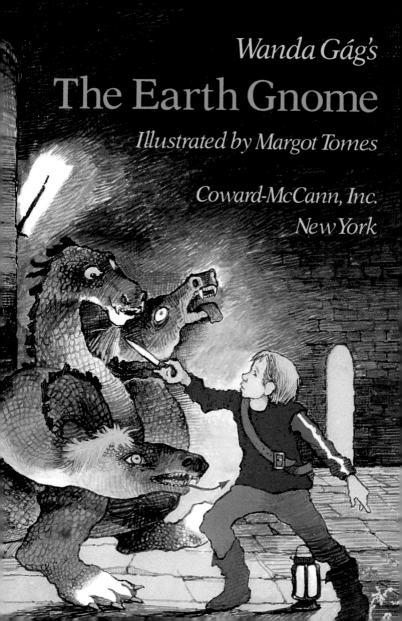

Wanda Gág's
The Earth Gnome

Illustrated by Margot Tomes

Coward-McCann, Inc.
New York

Published simultaneously in Canada by
General Publishing Co. Limited, Toronto.
Printed in Hong Kong.
Designed by Nanette Stevenson.
First printing.
Library of Congress Cataloging in Publication Data
Gág, Wanda,   Wanda Gág's The earth gnome.
Summary: An earth gnome helps a hunter boy
rescue three princesses who are trapped
underground by many-headed dragons.
[1. Fairy tales. 2. Folklore—Germany]
I. Tomes, Margot, ill. II. Title.
PZ8.G123 Ear 1985 [398.2'1'0943] [E] 84-23804
ISBN 0-698-20618-5

For my cousins
Francis and Dorrit Tomes

A rich King had three daughters who were the joy of his heart. The pride of his heart was a large palace park filled with beautiful flowers and handsome trees of many kinds. He was especially proud of his trees, and one in particular, an apple tree, was his favorite. So highly did he prize it that he allowed no one but himself to touch it.

"Anyone who lays hands on this apple tree will regret it," he said, "and whoever picks even one apple from it will be sent one hundred fathoms under the ground."

No one touched it, the apple tree flourished, and every fall its fruit became redder and fuller.

One year there came a harvest when the tree was so full of beautiful red apples that the tree was ready to break with the load, and its boughs hung down to the ground. The three young Princesses walked under the tree every day to see if the wind had blown down an apple, but never, never did they find one. At last the youngest Princess became so hungry for one of the round rosy apples that she said to her sisters, "Our father loves us too dearly to wish us at the bottom of the earth. I think he only meant that for strangers."

With this she plucked an apple and bit into it.

"Oh, taste this, my sisterkins," she said. "Now have I never in all my life tasted anything so good!"

The two other Princesses also bit into the apple, whereupon all three sank down into the earth so deep that no rooster ever crowed after them.

That noon when the King went out to fetch his daughters to the midday meal he could not find them. He called for them but they did not answer. He sent servants to

search the palace grounds—the children were not found. At last, grieved and troubled, he sent out a proclamation to his people.

"Whoever can find and bring back my three beloved daughters," he said, "shall have one of them for his wife."

At this hundreds of people went searching through the land, for the three girls were beloved by all because they had always been so friendly to everybody and were so beautiful besides.

Among the many who went forth on the search were three young hunter boys. For seven days they walked: looked here, looked there, found nothing. On the eighth day they came upon a big castle and, finding its doors open, they walked in and looked around. From one beautiful room to another they wandered until they came to

a great dining hall where stood a table set with sweet and savory food, still so warm that it was steaming. The three hunter boys, now hungrier than ever, sat down and looked at the tempting dishes, hoping that someone might come and invite them to dinner. For half a day they sat there but no one came. Then they searched from one end of the castle to the other but in it no living being was to be seen or heard.

When they returned to the dining hall and found the food still warm and steaming, they could bear it no longer. They sat down at the table and ate their fill. All went well—no one stopped them, the food tasted good, and they felt delightfully refreshed after the meal. Then, feeling strong and full of courage once more, they made plans to continue their search for the three Princesses.

"Since no one seems to be living in this castle at present," said the first, "we may as well make this our home for a while."

"And every day we'll draw lots for one of us to stay here and watch the castle," said the second, "while the other two go out on

the search. Do you agree, Dull Hansl?"

"Yes," said the youngest brother. Dull Hansl was not his real name but the two older brothers always called him that because they considered him dull and simple and because they didn't like him very well.

When the lots were drawn, it came out that the oldest brother would be the one to stay at home the following day.

The next morning the two younger brothers rose early, ate a good breakfast at the steaming table, then set out to try their luck.

The oldest brother stayed behind and kept careful watch over the castle but nothing happened until noontime. And then, who came? A little, little fellow—a gnome—came begging for a bit of bread to eat. The hunter took some bread off the table and cut a big slice all around the loaf. But when he handed it to the gnome, the little creature let it drop out of his hand and said, "Oh, now my bread has fallen to the floor! Wouldn't you please be so good as to pick it up for me?"

The hunter stooped down to pick up the bread, when whish! the gnome picked up a stick, grabbed the hunter by the hair and gave him a good beating. When he had done that, the gnome disappeared.

The next day it fell to the lot of the middle brother to stay at home but he fared no better than the first. That evening after the others had returned, he called his oldest brother aside and said, "Well, how did things go with you yesterday?"

"Oh, things went badly with me," said the oldest. "There came a little fellow who asked for bread; when I handed it to him he dropped it, and when I tried to pick it up for him the rascal thrashed me soundly."

"Just so it happened to me today," said the middle brother, "and what it all means, I don't know. But let's not say a work about it to Dull Hansl—he may as well have his troubles like the rest of us." And to this the oldest brother agreed.

On the third day, of course, it was Dull Hansl's turn to stay at home. There, at noontime, came the little gnome again, begging for a morsel of bread. Dull Hansl

cut a slice from the loaf which was lying on
the table and handed it to him. But the
little fellow let it drop and said as before,
"Oh, there goes my bread! Wouldn't you be
so good as to pick it up for me?"

"What?" cried Dull Hansl. "Can't you pick it up yourself? If you don't even want to take that much trouble for your daily bread, you don't deserve any either."

"You *must* do it!" shrieked the gnome, his small face red with fury.

For an answer Dull Hansl picked up the little rascal and gave him a thrashing.

"Stop! Stop!" yelled the gnome. "Let me go now, and I'll tell you where the three Princesses are."

"That's better!" said Dull Hansl and stopped. "Now sit down and tell me your story."

"I am an Earth Gnome," said the little one, "and of us there are more than a thousand. We live down inside of the earth and that is how I happened to know where the lost Princesses are. They ate one of their father's forbidden apples and so they sank one hundred fathoms down into the earth. And there they are still, inside of an old well in the King's palace garden. But it is an old forgotten well; there is no water in it."

"Thank you," said Dull Hansl. "And tomorrow you can take me and my brothers to this well, and then we will rescue the Princesses."

"No!" cried the gnome. "No, no! You must say nothing of this to your brothers. They do not like you and will not deal honestly by you. If you wish to free the Princesses, you must do it without your brothers."

"But I could never do it all alone," said Dull Hansl.

"If you do as I say, you will get other help," said the gnome. "Now then, get a big basket and let yourself be lowered into the

well. Take a bell with you, and don't forget your hunting knife, you'll need it! You'll need it for this reason: in the well are three rooms, and in each room there is one of the Princesses who has to sit there and comb the fleas out of the hair of a dragon with many heads. Those many heads you must cut off."

When the gnome had said these words he disappeared.

That evening when the two older brothers returned they said, "Well, Dull Hansl, how has it gone with you today?"

"Oh, so far so good," said Dull Hansl. "All day I have seen no living creature, only such a little man who came and asked for a piece of bread and then let it drop to the floor. When I wouldn't pick it up for him, the little thing began to scold me. Such a bold little rascal! But I showed him a thing or two. I thrashed him roundly

until he begged me to stop. After that he became right friendly and even told me where the three Princesses are hidden."

At this the other two turned green and yellow with anger, but then they said, "So where are the Princesses now?"

And did Dull Hansl tell them? Ah yes, he did. He forgot all about the gnome's warning and told them everything. At this his brothers were well pleased and began making plans for the morrow.

The next morning, after eating a hearty breakfast at the steaming table, all three journeyed forth to the King's orchard, and as soon as they reached it they drew lots as to who should first go down into the well. Again the lot fell to the oldest. So he took the bell and climbed into the basket, saying, "But as soon as I ring, you must pull me up immediately."

The two younger boys, after lowering the basket, waited and listened. It was not long before they heard a tinkling down below, so they pulled the basket up. The oldest brother stepped out of the basket, looking very pale. "I didn't like it down there," he said.

Next the middle brother tried it, but he too tinkled the bell before he was halfway down. When he stepped out of the basket he was trembling. "I saw no use in going all the way down," he said. "I think that gnome was lying anyway."

Now it was Dull Hansl's turn to go down.

"He won't go far," said the oldest brother after they had lowered the basket. "We'll hear his bell tinkle in a minute."

But they were wrong, for Dull Hansl allowed himself to be lowered to the very bottom of the well, one hundred fathoms under the ground. It was dark down there and far from pleasant, but Dull Hansl, seeing a door, took his hunting knife, stepped out of the basket, and listened at the keyhole.

All he heard was a loud threefold snore.

"That is not the snore of a human being,"

he thought. "No doubt it comes from one of the dragons, and I may as well get to work on him."

Slowly he opened the door and peered in. There in a cave-like room was a dragon, sound asleep and snoring mightily. His heads, three of them, were resting on the lap of the oldest Princess, and she was busy combing his hair.

Dull Hansl, losing no time, raised his hunting knife, and:

Whack! Whack! Whack!

The dragon's three heads were off and lying on the floor. The Princess jumped up, hugged and kissed him, and thanked him for freeing her. So grateful was she that she even took off her stomacher of pure gold and hung it around his neck.

Now Dull Hansl opened the door of the second room, and there he saw a medium-sized dragon, also sound asleep and snoring even louder than the first. This one had

seven heads and his hair was combed by
the second Princess. Dull Hansl raised his
hunting knife and:

Whack! Whack! Whack!
Whack! Whack! Whack!
WHACK!

Off went the dragon's seven heads and fell to the floor. The second Princess jumped up and thanked him, and then Dull Hansl went on and opened the third door. In that room was the youngest Princess combing the hair of a very big dragon. He was a dragon with nine heads and he was sleeping soundly and shaking the earth with his ninefold snores.

Dull Hansl was glad to see him so sound asleep and lost no time. He raised his hunting knife, and:

Whack! Whack! Whack!
Whack! Whack! Whack!
Whack!
Whack!
WHACK!

Off went the nine heads of the biggest dragon. At this the three Princesses were so happy that they crowded around Dull Hansl and hugged and kissed him without stopping.

Now that all the Princesses were free, it was time to get them up to the earth again.

Dull Hansl placed the oldest Princess in
the basket and tinkled the bell so loudly
that his brother above heard it and pulled
her up. Next the second Princess was
drawn up, and then the third.

Finally it was Dull Hansl's turn to be pulled up but now, at last, just as he was about to step into the basket, he remembered that the gnome had warned him against his brothers.

"First I will try them out to see if they mean to do right by me," he thought, and so he picked up a heavy rock and put it in the basket. Then he tinkled the bell.

The two older brothers tugged at the basket until it was halfway up to the earth, then cut the rope so that the basket fell back into the well. It made a loud thud, at which the two brothers were pleased, for now, thinking that they were rid of their youngest brother, they planned to claim the reward for themselves. But before they consented to take the Princesses back to their father, the two false brothers made them promise they would never tell a living being how they had been saved.

While the brothers were presenting themselves to the King as his daughters' rescuers, Dull Hansl was wandering sadly around in the three rooms in the bottom of the well.

"Now what shall I do?" he said. "The rope is cut, my brothers are gone—I shall be left to starve down here, no doubt."

He saw a flute hanging on the wall. "Oh flute," he said, "why are you hanging there? No one would be merry enough to play a tune on you in this dismal place!"

He looked at the dragons' heads too, saying, "And you can't help me either."

All night he walked, back and forth, forth and back, and did it so many times that the earth floor became smooth and shiny from his footsteps. But in the morning, as he passed the flute again and again, he began to get an idea. "That flute seems to be there for something," he thought. "I'll blow on it and see what happens."

So he took the flute and blew on it. And what happened? Dozens of little earth gnomes appeared from all around him! With each note he played, another gnome came; and he blew and blew on that flute until the room was crammed with the tiny creatures.

"What is your wish?" asked the many little gnomes in many little voices. "We are here to do your bidding."

"Oh, I would dearly love to be back up on the earth in the good daylight," said Dull Hansl.

"It shall be done," said the many little gnomes. With this, they all took hold of him, one little gnome on each hair of his head, and in that way they flew up to the earth into the good daylight with him. And as soon as Dull Hansl was up there, the gnomes vanished.

Dull Hansl now went to the King's palace, arriving there just as the oldest brother was about to be wed to the oldest Princess. He appeared before the King and his three daughters, but as soon as the three Princesses set eyes on their true rescuer, they all fell into a faint.

The King became very angry at the poor boy.

"Throw this newcomer into the dungeon!" he cried to his servants. "See—he has hurt or bewitched my dear daughters, the sorcerer!"

At this Dull Hansl was taken away and

locked up in the dungeon. But as soon as the three Princesses recovered their senses and heard what had happened, they rushed up to the King and asked him to change his mind about the newcomer.

"Please free him, father," said the first Princess.

"He did not hurt us—he is good," said the second.

"But why do you say this?" asked the King. "Have you seen him before?"

The Princesses looked at each other, and then the youngest said, "That is something we cannot tell you, father. We promised never to tell it to any living being."

"If you have promised that," said their father, "I will not ask you to tell me. But why don't you go out into the kitchen and tell it to the stove? That is not a living being."

The three Princesses ran out into the kitchen, closed the door, and told the stove that it was Dull Hansl, and not his brothers, who had freed them and killed all the dragons. And did the stove hear it? I don't know. But the King, who stood outside the kitchen door, heard every word of it, and I am sure you can guess the rest!

The two brothers were punished for their wickedness and Dull Hansl was allowed to choose one of the Princesses for his wife. He liked them all, but he chose the youngest because she was just his age, and so they were married and lived happily ever after.